TOO NOISY!

Listen while I tell you
all about a bunch of Bungles –
they're a great enormous family
and they're noisy,
oh so noisy!

For Lucy ～ M. D.

For Florence and Nell ～ E. V.

TOO NOISY!

malachy doyle
ed vere

WALKER BOOKS
AND SUBSIDIARIES
LONDON · BOSTON · SYDNEY · AUCKLAND

FIRST PUBLISHED 2012 BY WALKER BOOKS LTD, 87 VAUXHALL WALK, LONDON SE11 5HJ • 10 9 8 7 6 5 4 3 2 1 • TEXT © 2012 MALACHY DOYLE • ILLUSTRATIONS © 2012 ED VERE • THE RIGHT OF MALACHY DOYLE AND ED VERE TO BE IDENTIFIED AS AUTHOR AND ILLUSTRATOR RESPECTIVELY OF THIS WORK HAS BEEN ASSERTED BY THEM IN ACCORDANCE WITH THE COPYRIGHT, DESIGNS AND PATENTS ACT 1988 • THIS BOOK HAS BEEN TYPESET IN NEUTRAFACE MEDIUM ALT AND BODONI ANTIQUA T DEMI BOLD • PRINTED IN CHINA • ALL RIGHTS RESERVED • NO PART OF THIS BOOK MAY BE REPRODUCED, TRANSMITTED OR STORED IN AN INFORMATION RETRIEVAL SYSTEM IN ANY FORM OR BY ANY MEANS, GRAPHIC, ELECTRONIC OR MECHANICAL, INCLUDING PHOTOCOPYING, TAPING AND RECORDING, WITHOUT PRIOR WRITTEN PERMISSION FROM THE PUBLISHER • BRITISH LIBRARY CATALOGUING IN PUBLICATION DATA: A CATALOGUE RECORD FOR THIS BOOK IS AVAILABLE FROM THE BRITISH LIBRARY • ISBN 978-1-4063-1945-3
• WWW.MALACHYDOYLE.COM • WWW.EDVERE.COM • WWW.WALKER.CO.UK

CRASH! JANGLE!

Meet the Bungles –

Whistle! Tweetle! Toot!

Mama Bungle *trills* and *tinkles*,

Papa **wheezes,** then he **sneezes,**

Granny Bungle *clicks* and *clacks*

and Grandpa Bill's a **boomer,**

Bella **bangs** on pots and pans

and Fitz and Finn,

the Bunglebabies,

Squeak and

Squawk and

SQUELCH!

"Oh, will you ever shush!" cried Sam,
the middle one, the quiet one,
the Bungle full of dreams.
"There isn't room to think round here,
all boom and bash and wallop!
Oh, I want it to be peaceful
but it's not – it never is!"

And so he upped

and so he offed

and so he wandered

to the wood.

"Aha!" he sighed,
"that's better," as he
looked around at clouds
and trees and greens
and blues and water.

He sat and looked,
and thought and looked,
and sat and hummed
a hum.

*"The sky is blue.
My shoe is, too!"*

"It rhymes!" said Sam.
"I like it!"

He had another little walk ...
then sat and looked,
and thought and looked,
and sat and hummed again.

"I can see a funny tree.
Stripy, just like Mama B!"

"It rhymes!" said Sam.
"I love it!"

Sam upped

and offed

and wandered

deeper, deep into the wood.

But *"Eeek!"* – he felt a creepy-crawly climbing up his trouser leg.

"Oooh," he said. "It's dark," he said. "I think I might be lost," he said.

Then **"Beek!"**
– he felt a flitter-flutter
flap around his face!
"Oooh," he said.
"I'm scared," he said.
"I wished I hadn't dared,"
he said, "go off alone,
all on my own."

Then

"*Eeeky-beek!*"

– a slippy-slidy
slithered
down his neck!

He opened up his lips

and then he opened up his mouth

and then he opened

up his throat

and *bellowed,*

Help!

Help!

He listened
and he listened
and ...

well, first
Sam heard a *little* sound –
a *trilling* and a *tinkling* ...

then he heard a bigger sound –
a **wheezing** and a **sneezing** ...

a **clicking** and a **clacking**,

then a **boomty-boomty-booming,**

growing **loud and loud again**

till it was like a ...

HURRICANE
of lovely NOISE!

The sun came through the trees
and so did Mama Bungle, Papa Bungle,
Grandpa Bill and Granny, too,
Bella banging pots and pans
and Fitz and Finn, the Bunglebabies –
Squeak, **Squawk**, **SQUELCH!**

"It's Sam," they yelled,
"we've found him!"

And they gathered all around him,
and they hugged him and they kissed him,
and they said how much they'd missed him.
He said he'd missed them too,
he said ...

"Although you're very loud,
you crowd, I'm glad to be a Bungle!"

Well, everybody cheered,
"HOORAY!"

And Sam was oh so happy,
for he loved them, every one.

"Quiet's good..." said Mama B.
"It is," said Sam, and nodded.
"But noisy's good as well sometimes –
especially when you're lost!"

*And that's the ending,
happy ending.*

That's the end.